Steve Webb

Tanka Tanka Skunk!

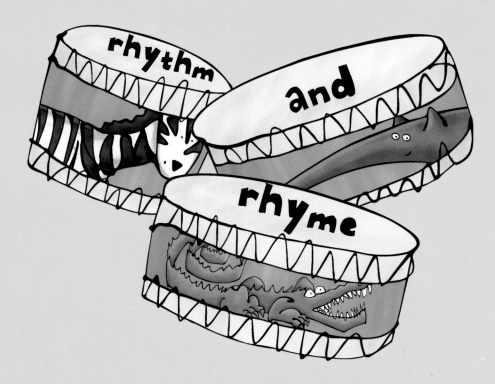

rhythm and rhyme

Orchard Books ⊚ New York
An Imprint of Scholastic Inc.

This is
Tanka

This is

SKUNK

They love to play the drums.

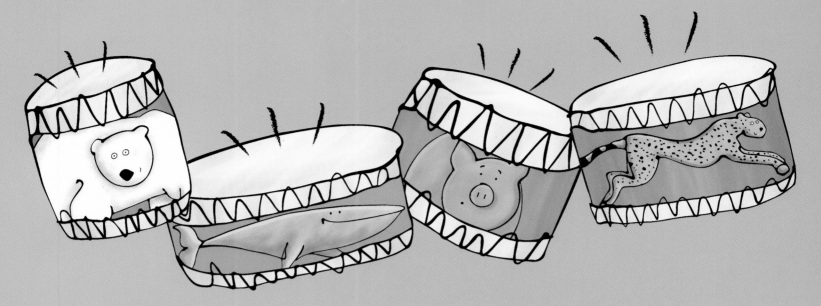

Say their names together,

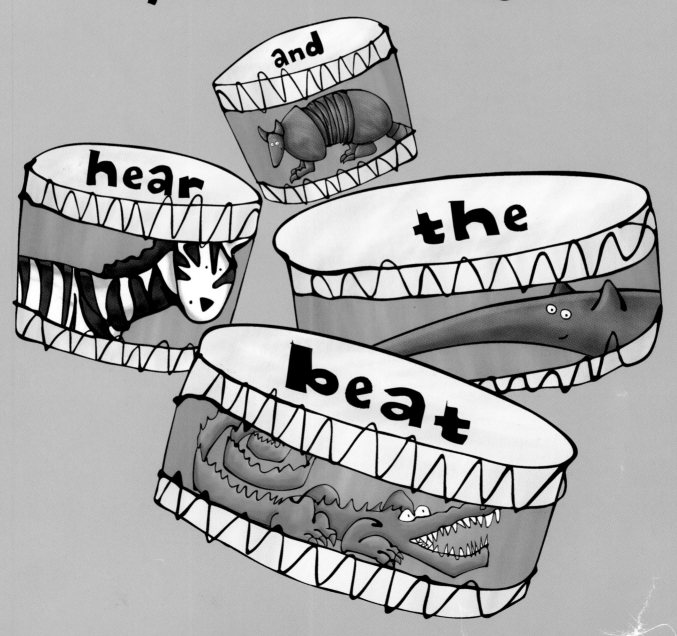

and

hear

the

beat

like this...

Skunka Tanka

Skunka Tanka

Tanka
Tanka
Skunk!

This is kangaroo.
His name has
three beats.

And this is caterpillar.
His name has
four beats.

tiger

cheetah

tiger

cheetah

panda

polar
bear

lemur

llama

llama

lemur

zebra

badger

BAT

cat- er- pil- lar

BIG GORILLA

YAKETY YAKETY YAK

dingo

donkey

DUCK

panda

panther

tiger

zebra

alligator

FOX

tiny

little

hairy

spider

armadillo

ox

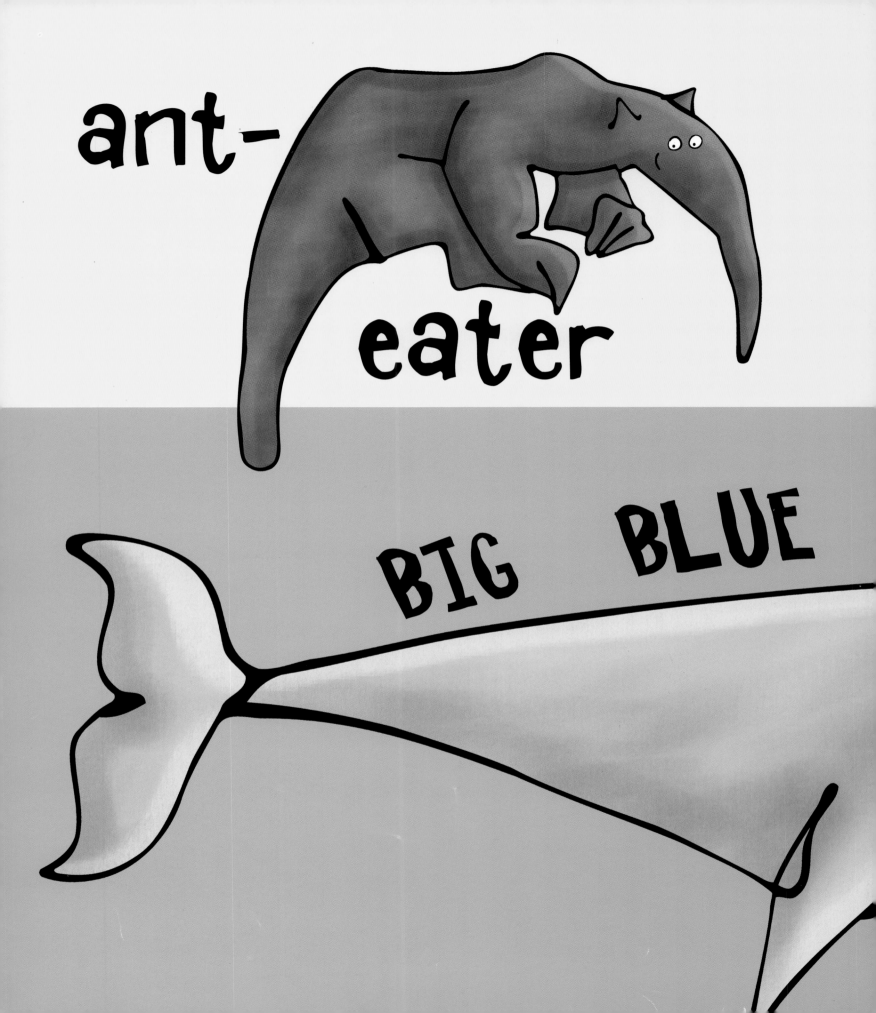

Once more from the top. . .

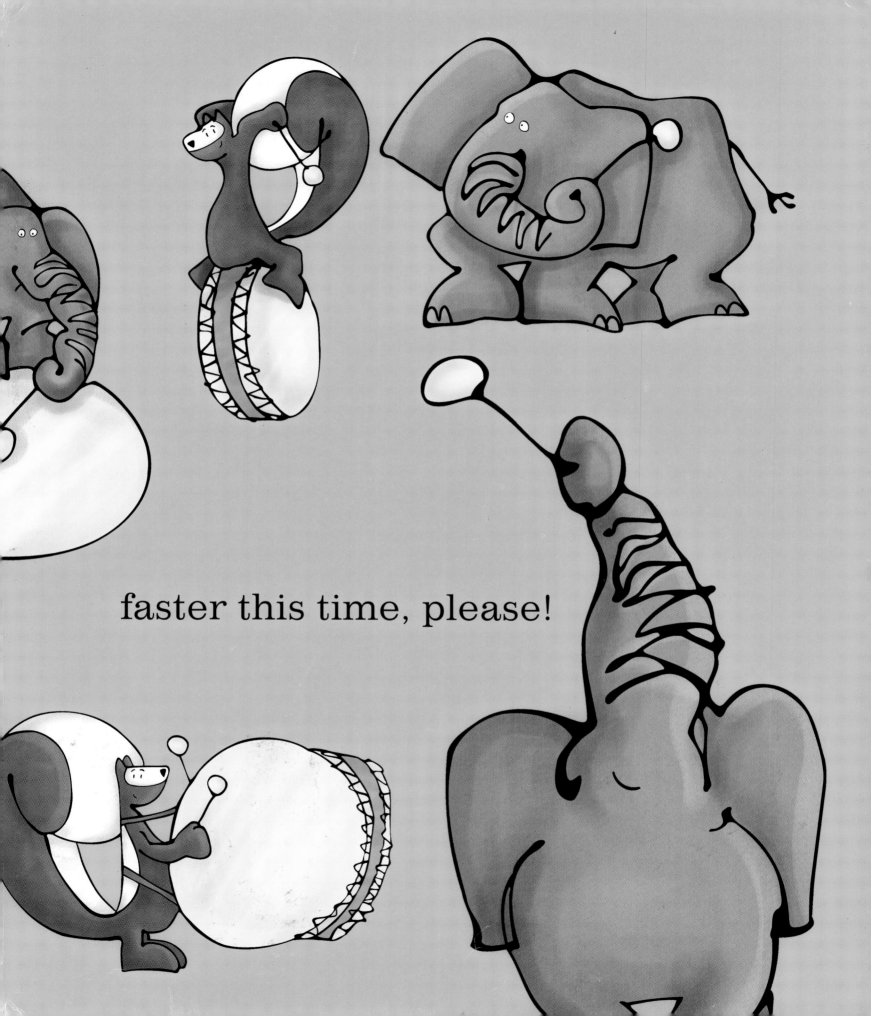

faster this time, please!

For my very favorite people
in all the world,
Sam, Hannah, and Kate.
Hats off to Ernie,
and "bonsoir" to Badger...

Library of Congress Cataloging-in-Publication Data available

ISBN 0-439-57844-2

10 9 8 7 6 5 4 3 2 1   04 05 06 07 08
First Scholastic edition, July 2004
Reinforced Binding for Library Use

Printed in China